Little Bear

For Uncle Ray and Auntie Gill

SIMON & SCHUSTER

First published in Great Britain in 2021 by Simon & Schuster UK Ltd, 1st Floor, 222 Gray's Inn Road, London WC1X 8HB

A CIP catalogue record for this book is available from the British Library upon request

ISBN: 978-1-3985-0248-2 (HB)
ISBN: 978-1-3985-0250-5 (eBook)

Printed in China
1 3 5 7 9 10 8 6 4 2

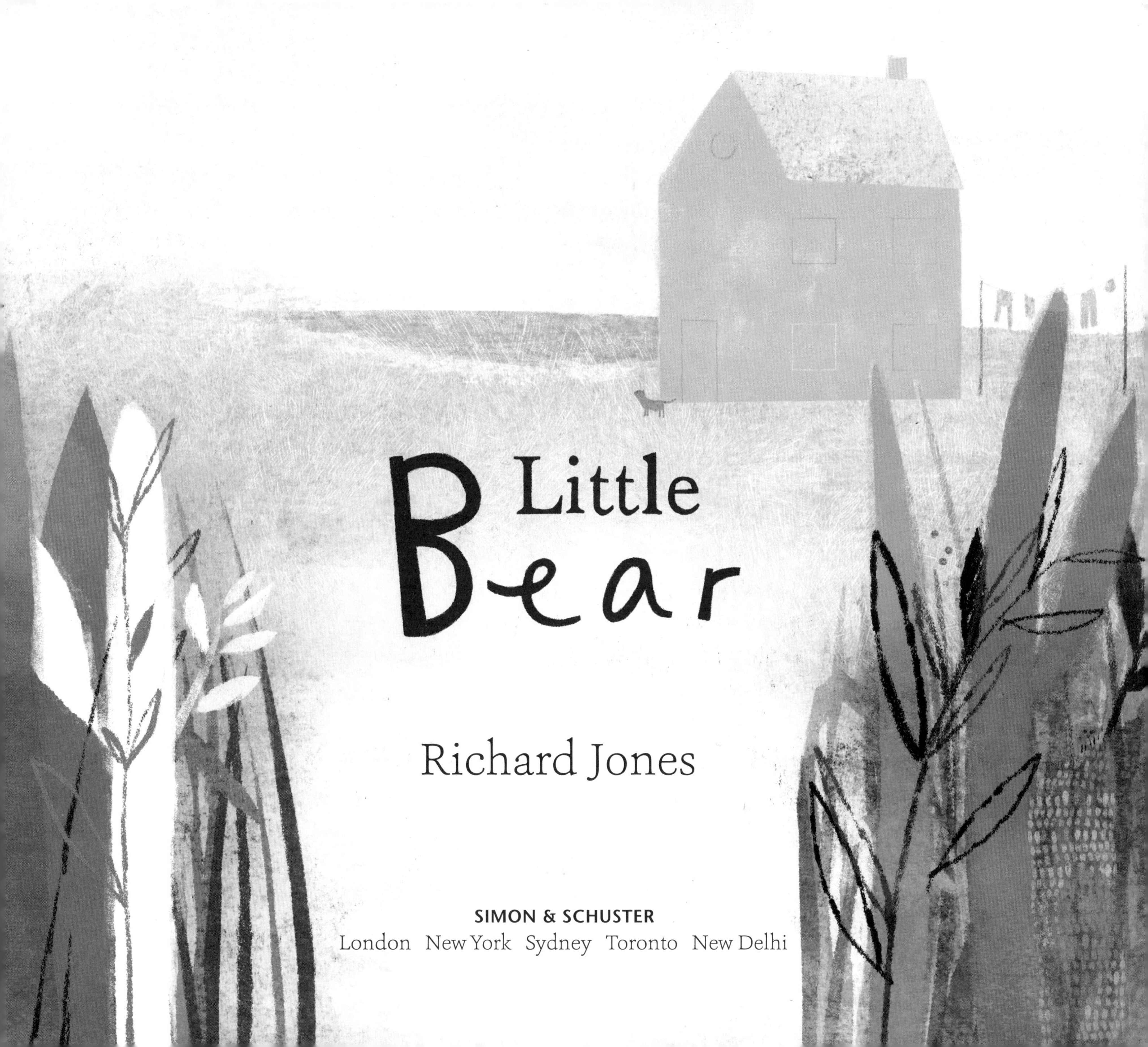

Little Bear

Richard Jones

SIMON & SCHUSTER
London New York Sydney Toronto New Delhi

On **Monday,** I found a polar bear in the garden.

He was so small, I held him in my hands.

I could feel his heart beating beneath his cloud-white fur.
His black paws were warm and rough against my skin.

"Are you lost, little bear?" I asked. "Can I help you?"

On **Tuesday**, he had grown too big to hold in my hands.
So I popped him in my pocket.

"You're safe now, little bear.
Don't be scared."

We played together all afternoon.

On **Wednesday**, he had grown too big for my pocket!
So I put him in my hat.

"I think it's time to take you home, little bear."

“Raise the anchor!

Set the sail!

Away we go!”

On **Thursday**, he had grown too big for my hat . . .
So he curled up tightly, safe and warm in my bag.

"Goodnight, little bear. Sleep tight."

I held the bag close as we sailed
through the night.

On **Friday**, he had grown too big for my bag.
So he climbed up onto my shoulders.
His soft whiskers tickled my neck.

"Hold on tight, little bear!"

The wind pushed and pulled at our red sails,
and green waves lifted us up, up, up into the frozen air.

Then back down,

down,

down we went.

Birds made circles in the sky and all the while,
the kind sun kept us warm.

On **Saturday**, he had grown too big for my shoulders.
So he jumped down into the boat beside me.

"Don't fall in, little bear. We'll be there soon!"

On **Sunday**, he had grown too big for the boat!
So I climbed up onto *his* back.

"Land ahoy, little bear!"

We played together all day!

But the sky soon grew dark and the silver stars began to shine once more. I wanted to stay with him forever,

but it was time to sail home.

"Goodbye, little bear, goodbye.

See you again soon."